BEN TUCKE
MOUNTAIN M

THE WAY WEST

BOOK TWO

ROBERT HANLON

Copyright © 2020 by Robert Hanlon

Published by DS Productions

ISBN: 9798685262363

ACKNOWLEDGEMENT

TO MY WIFE, FOR ACCEPTING MY MISTRESS—
WRITING.

INSPIRATION

You won't know love until you give away love, and the greatest gift of love is to give of yourself without expecting anything in return.

No politician can resist making promises they can't keep.

Lies travel faster than the truth and are much harder to kill.

Your biggest critic is the person looking back at you from the mirror.

Sometimes it takes more courage to walk away than to stand and fight.

Everyone is weird in their own way, and some are more than others.

In sales it is far better to be an invited guest than an unwanted pest. Advertise, and let them call you.

CHAPTER ONE

Tuck didn't look back as he rode off down the trail. He felt betrayed by Bonnie. They'd made a deal, and she went back on her word. He was angry with her, but he could not bring himself to keep on riding and never come back. She had suggested he offer his services as a scout to the army. He had to admit it was a good fit for his skill set, though he hated the idea of asking for the job when it was her idea.

He was approaching the fort's command quarters, still debating with himself over the idea, when Major Newton (Newt) Jennings stepped out the door.

When he looked up, he saw Tuck riding by and shouted, "Tuck, Tuck, can I have a word with you?" He hurried down the steps onto the parade grounds. Tuck pulled up on the reins and stopped.

"What can I do for you, Major?" Tuck asked.

"I have need for a scout—someone with real knowledge of the territory and plenty of grit. Everybody says the man I need is you," Jennings said.

"A scout, Major? Did Bonnie put you up to this?" Tuck asked.

"No, sir. I wouldn't think she'd understand what I need in a scout. Aside from that, what do you say? Will you scout for us?" the major pressed.

"I might consider it if I have some real control over the troops I lead," Tuck replied.

"Of course, you'll work closely with the officer in charge," the major countered.

"Let me make it clear for you, Major. You haven't got a single man, let alone an officer, who has been west of the Mississippi or seen action against Indians. I'm willing to bet there are at least a half-dozen Indian braves in among the rocks and trees overlooking this valley, keeping an eye on you and this town. Unless you know the territory and a good deal about the Indians who claim this area and the areas you will be traveling through, the best you can hope for is to die quickly," Tuck stated curtly.

"Now, if you want me to scout for you, I will, if I'm in charge, and your troopers and tenderfoot officers are ordered to live and learn under my command. I have no intention of losing my scalp following some inexperienced wet-behind-the-ears officer.

"You can't send inexperienced children out into the wilderness and expect them to survive. The natives in this territory are not the friendliest, and they will not hesitate to kill every man you send out to have a look around," Tuck explained, painting a dismal picture.

"I can't just enlist you as a captain, Tuck. The army has rules and regulations."

"It's not if, Major, but when those men will die. And you're wrong to think your men will learn as they go because they won't live long enough," Tuck explained.

"Why don't you sleep on it, and we'll talk in the morning," Major Jennings suggested. "I'll have the sergeant set you up in the guest quarters."

"Much obliged," Tuck replied. It sure beat sleeping on the ground.

The following morning, Tuck was up at dawn, along with the entire contingent building the new fort. Tuck was directed to the

2

officers' mess where he was served biscuits and gravy, eggs, bacon, toast, and hot coffee. It was good, and Tuck was nearly sold on the idea of joining the army rather than just scouting for them. However, he changed his mind when he remembered he would be forced to live where the army sent him, and he wouldn't be able to come and go as he saw fit.

Tuck ate breakfast with two young lieutenants who were behaving as though Tuck was an incredible leader of some sort. They were both acting a bit strange. They were polite and friendly, but their conversation was stiff and stilted.

"They say mountain men are tough as nails and smart as whips. Do you find that to be true?" Lieutenant Milner asked. Tuck was naturally wary of strangers and began to get that feeling Jefferson had always counseled him to pay attention to. He'd also taught Tuck to only provide information on a need-to-know basis, and even then to be stingy.

"There are a few tough ones and a few smart ones, but the combination of smart and tough, well, I imagine it's about the same in any walk of life. There are some, but not an overabundance of them. Common sense isn't all that common," Tuck replied.

The two lieutenants shared a glance, then Lieutenant Beckwith asked, "So, which do you view yourself as—smart or tough?" Tuck took another mouthful of food while looking for any sign that the two lieutenants were pulling his leg, funnin' with him.

"Gentlemen, I'd like to make a suggestion to the two of you that will serve you well as you travel about the West, or even upon your return back East. You need to be cognizant of the fact that asking certain questions may cause the person you have asked the question of to feel you're trying to poke fun at them. As one deals with his fellow man on a regular basis, if you've got the reputation of being crass and conceited, you may find the answers you receive may tend to be more physical than verbal. We mountain men don't suffer fools well, especially if those fools haven't a clue just how uneducated and foolish they are." Tuck concluded and finished off his breakfast. As he got up to leave, the two lieutenants stood as well and quickly stepped up to Tuck, boxing him in.

"You know, Tuck, if we didn't know better, we would think you've taken offense to our friendly inquiries. That is hardly the behavior of a military man when dealing with his superiors," Lieutenant Milner stated in his most intimidating tone as he leaned forward toward Tuck.

Tuck quickly ascertained that the two lieutenants were trying to establish themselves as the top dogs in the pack. He had no interest in competing with the two childish junior officers, but he figured the two of them needed a lesson in manners just the same. "Gentlemen, I don't have the time to play games with you this morning, so I would appreciate you stepping aside and letting me pass," he said politely.

Lieutenant Beckwith, who was standing behind him, grabbed Tuck's shoulders. Tuck let his body go limp, and he dropped out of Beckwith's grip just as Milner threw a punch meant to hit Tuck in the face. Milner ended up hitting Beckwith, causing him to stagger.

Tuck delivered a gut-wrenching blow to Milner, doubling him over. Then, in a continuous, smooth-flowing motion, he swung back at Beckwith, delivering a second, more powerful blow to the man's face, blackening both eyes and breaking his nose. Milner was attempting to get back in the fight as Tuck spun around and smashed the china plate he'd eaten breakfast on into Milner's chin, which sent Milner to the floor, out cold, blood rushing out of the corner of his mouth.

Tuck stood there, shaking his head at the two immature and inexperienced fools being passed off as army officers until he finally made up his mind as to exactly what he would require if he decided to help the army.

As he stepped past Beckwith, who was leaning over, letting the blood drip out of his nose, Tuck said, "To answer your question if mountain men are tough or smart, we are both. Let me know if you and Milner want another lesson. We can do breakfast after the two of you heal up. Oh, and by the way, I hardly consider you my superior. I'm not in the army; I'm a civilian, and if you're in the army, that means you work for me." Tuck continued to the door.

At the door of the mess hall, Tuck was greeted by a Sergeant O'Reilly. "There you are, sir. Major Jennings would like a word with you before you leave," the sergeant said. The sergeant couldn't help but notice the two young officers, now sitting in chairs, looking as though they had been trampled in a stampede. "What happened to them?" he asked Tuck.

"They had a disagreement about whether it was better to be smart than tough, or vice versa. I think it was decided—you need to be both tough and smart if you're going to survive out here in the West." Tuck stepped through the door and walked off toward the post commander's office. The sergeant followed a step or two behind Tuck.

"Do you think I should send a couple of troopers to help them to the medical tent?" the sergeant asked.

"By all means," Tuck replied. "I'd send four men with stretchers, in case they are unable to walk." Tuck smirked as he climbed up the steps to the porch in front of the major's office door.

"Yes, sir, I'll get on that right away," Sergeant O'Reilly replied. He walked off, briskly shouting orders at a handful of troopers as he went.

Tuck reached the door to the major's office and knocked. A moment later he heard a muffled, "Come in," and he stepped inside. Major Jennings was leaning over a table with a captain who looked to be just slightly older than himself or the young lieutenants.

"Good morning, Tuck. I don't believe you've met Captain Colton Daniels. He'll be the man in charge of the contingent moving to the Grand Junction Trading Post. He'll be taking one hundred men and supplies there to establish a fort and bring some stability to the area. Any thoughts on the subject or pointers you might be willing to give?" the major asked.

"What trail are you thinking of following?" Tuck asked as he stepped over to the table to look at the map.

"We understand there are two trails that will take us to Grand Junction from here. Which is the better route?" the captain asked.

"Better is an interesting yet relative word to try to describe either of the trails. Each one has advantages and disadvantages," Tuck replied.

"Yes, so, which one is the better of the two?" Captain Daniels repeated, apparently not understanding or choosing not to listen to Tuck's comment that "better" didn't really apply to his question.

"Okay, I'll try to make this clearer for you. The word better doesn't apply in this situation. Neither trail is better than the other—just less bad," Tuck said.

"This is utter nonsense—better doesn't apply. Is English your first language, or is it something else?" the captain snapped.

"Captain, mind your manners, or you'll find yourself on report," Major Jennings snarled.

"Yes, sir," the captain quickly responded. "I apologize, fine sir."

"Now, Tuck, will you please get to the point?" the major said.

"Certainly, Major. Both trails twist, turn, rise, and fall. The trails tend to be used by the Indians, as there is little commerce between Leadville and Grand Junction because these trails are so bad. They are both thin and in rugged terrain. In places, the trail is barely wide enough for one horse. Neither will support a wagon. The Indians use them primarily for hunting parties of three or four braves," Tuck explained.

"The better route is the same route you came in on. Follow the White River northwest to the open plain, then turn southwest for five days."

"There's nothing shorter?" the captain pressed.

"No. Going any other way forces you into tight passes, steep ravines, loose shale mountainsides, and into terrain the Arapaho and Comanches have lived and hunted on for a thousand years," Tuck said. He added, "Putting you at a distinct disadvantage."

"But we're a modern army with the latest firearms, and we're all well trained and capable," the captain boasted. "We need to be in Grand Junction in five days from tomorrow."

"If you go the way you're thinking of going with a large contingent of men, you're asking for trouble," Tuck told him.

7

"I appreciate your opinion, sir, but I have orders. I have yet to fail in fulfilling my orders, and I shall not start now," the captain said, dismissing Tuck's advice and experience.

"Was there something else you wanted to see me about, Major?" Tuck asked.

"I was wondering if you'd changed your mind since last night?" the major asked.

"I have," Tuck replied.

"Oh, good." The major smiled, thinking he'd recruited one of the best hunter-trackers in the territory.

"I don't know if I'd go that far, Major," Tuck said.

"What?"

"I have changed my mind. I will only accept the position of scout if on each trek I take for the army, I am temporarily appointed to the rank of major, and I am the sole leader of the expedition. My orders override all other orders for the expedition or anyone involved. The captain's refusal to accept the information I've provided regarding the expedition he's about to take proves to me that if I settle for anything less, the army will get me killed," Tuck stated bluntly. "Now, if there isn't anything else, I've got a long ride back to my cabin."

As Tuck turned away, Captain Daniels turned to Major Jennings and said, "That is a ridiculous demand. Just who does he think he is?"

"He's the best man in the territory, according to every man I've spoken with," the major replied.

Then, just as Tuck reached to open the door, it swung open, and in charged the two young lieutenants.

"Stop that man and arrest him!" Milner shouted. "He attacked us."

Tuck just shook his head and continued to step through the door.

"Grab him!" Beckwith shouted, and the sergeant who had accompanied Tuck from the officers' mess held up his hands and let Tuck pass. "What are you doing, Sergeant? Arrest that man!" Beckwith wailed.

"What is the meaning of this?" Major Jennings demanded.

"He attacked us. The sergeant saw him do it," said Milner, sounding a bit like he was drunk, slurring his words through his swollen jaw.

"Sergeant, is that true?" the major asked.

"I couldn't say, sir. When I picked up Mr. Tuck, he was leaving the mess, and the two lieutenants were sitting in chairs opposite each other. I asked Mr. Tuck what happened. He said the lieutenants had an argument over whether mountain men were tough or smart. His opinion was they were both. If there was a fight involving Mr. Tuck, they must not have laid a hand on him, because he didn't have a drop of blood on him—anywhere," Sergeant O'Reilly explained.

Tuck had walked back to the door, and after the sergeant finished talking, Tuck stated loudly, "There's no charge for the schooling, Major." He then walked away to get his horse.

Robert Hanlon

CHAPTER TWO

As Tuck rode out of the fort, he didn't bother to look back. Captain Daniels stood on the porch outside the major's office, trying to convince the major that he had enough experience to lead the expedition. After a spirited debate, Captain Daniels won the argument, although there really hadn't been any other conclusion the major could reach. After all, we are talking about the United States Army and its regulations.

Captain Daniels gathered the troops and made a change regarding the handling of the supplies. Instead of taking twenty big heavy wagons packed with supplies, he chose to follow one of Tuck's recommendations and not take any wagons, due to the apparent roughness of the trail. Instead, he would take every mule the army could commandeer—about twenty—plus two dozen pack horses. The following morning, Captain Daniels left the fort with a contingent of one hundred twenty men and one hundred forty-four animals. They took the trail to the south-southwest, the one Tuck had strongly recommended they not take at all.

Tuck rode into the mountains to the north of Leadville. He crossed the White River just west of the head waters of the river at Turquoise Lake, so named for the abundance of the semi-precious stones found in and around the lake. Tuck was looking for bighorn sheep and deer. He wanted to harvest them for meat and for their hides. Both brought top dollar at the trading posts, as they made fine coats and leggings for the winter months and were above-average eating year round.

Tuck wasn't used to hunting alone, or being alone, for that matter. Since Jefferson had rescued him from those Kansa Indians, back on the edge of the plains when his parents had been killed, he'd only spent a few hours alone now and then. Jefferson had been his constant companion, his friend, and mentor. He owed him so much, and now he could never even attempt to repay him.

For three days, even though he was hunting, Tuck didn't do much more than scout the game trails and sit looking at the mountains. It was on the third day, while he sat grieving the loss of Jefferson, that he spotted a dark line moving across the valley floor below.

Last year, at Fort Collins, he had traded for a looking glass. The man he traded with claimed he got it from a ship's captain in New Orleans. When held up against your eye, something or someone up to a mile or two away would suddenly seem as though they were only a few yards away, and you could almost touch them. Tuck took the looking glass from his saddlebag and peered through it at the dark line in the valley.

It was as clear as a spring morning in the Rockies; the dark line was a hunting party of Arapaho Indians, and they were headed south. He counted twenty braves and four ponies strung behind them for carrying game. Tuck decided he needed to follow them to see where they were going. He followed them the rest of the day—right back to Leadville.

CHAPTER THREE

As night fell, Tuck had a real conundrum to deal with. The Arapaho had stopped and spread out across the face of the mountain. While Tuck was watching them, he realized he had seriously miscalculated their number. Suddenly, the twenty braves became fifty, and the way they were setting up, he could see that they were going to attack the settlers while forming a defensive line to hold back the army or blue bellies as long as possible. That would give the other braves time to kill as many settlers as possible.

Tuck needed to warn the town and the fort, but how? He couldn't exactly ride down the mountain, passing through the savages, without becoming a human pin cushion for their arrows. In looking down at the town and the fort, the only thing that jumped out at him was the campfires that were set in several places to provide light and ward off mountain lions and bears. There were a lot of grizzly bears in these mountains.

As he watched the Arapaho continue to spread out and work their way down the mountain, which was more like a six-hundred-foot-high pile of broken rocks, it occurred to Tuck there was a way to alert the men at the fort and in the town. The brush was extremely dry this year. Although there wasn't much of the dried-out brush, there was enough to catch fire quickly, burn brightly, and cause someone to sound the alarms in town and at the fort.

Tuck quickly collected enough dried-out brush to create five big mounds. He piled the brush right at the edge of the mountainside. Then he grabbed his rope and ran a couple loops of rope around each of the five mounds. He left enough rope on each mound to allow him to whip it and toss it over the mountainside. Then he made sure all six of the rifles he carried were loaded and ready to fire.

Knowing that time was running out, Tuck took out his flint and began making small fires under each mound of brush. By the time he had gotten all five ignited, the first mound had burst into flames. Tuck quickly ran back to the flaming mound, grabbed the rope, and began twirling the burning brush around his head five times. Then he flung it over the edge.

The bundle of burning brush arched high into the air and then plummeted down the side of the mountain before smashing into the mountainside. The brush showered the area around it with embers and burning branches, setting other small fires in the tinder-dry clumps of brush.

Tuck repeated the flaming lariat toss four more times with the same results, igniting small fires everywhere. The night guards at the fort weren't sure what they were seeing, but they were smart enough to realize something was wrong. They sounded the alarm, and Major Jennings was so concerned, he called out the entire troop. All but forty men took to their horses and charged up the valley to the town and the burning brush on the mountainside. The forty men left at the fort were ordered to defend it.

Tuck smiled when he heard the bugler signaling charge. Then he saw a dark wave of what he assumed were the cavalry coming to the rescue of the town. Tuck looked down the mountain as the Indians began pulling back and moving around the mountain. That would make it appear that they had never been there. Tuck wasn't about to let that happen. He put the first of his rifles to his shoulder, aimed, and fired.

A brave sneaking behind a large boulder suddenly spun around, slammed into the boulder, and dropped to the ground. Tuck shot three more braves before the Indians realized there was a shooter above them on the mountain top. The cavalry had arrived below, where the brush fires were, and began seeing the occasional Indian dart between boulders. The major ordered half his men to form a picket line and begin moving up the hill after the Indians. Tuck made his last two shots count, and then it was a race against time to reload at least one gun before the savages crested the mountain.

The sergeant ordered to clear the mountainside of hostiles, led the charge, and to his and his troopers' consternation, they quickly discovered not all the Indians were escaping. The first surprised Indian attack occurred a third of the way up the mountain. An Indian surprised a trooper checking out the area around a huge boulder. The trooper was slowly making his way around the barn-sized boulder when he reached a squared-off corner. As he stepped around the corner, he heard a sound behind him. It sounded as if someone may have kicked a rock. He turned his head to look behind him, and that was when the Indian struck.

The Indian lunged out from his hiding place and jammed a big stone knife into the left side of the trooper's chest. It killed him instantly, and it happened so fast that the man never saw the Indian who killed him.

The second attack occurred ten yards away. This time, there were two troopers working in tandem to flush out the savages. These boulders were smaller. They could still hide a man, but there were gaps and dips in the stones. Looking in the right place at the right time, the movements of an adversary were visible through the gaps. One of the troopers took point ten yards out, and the second trooper was charged with providing his cover.

The right place at the right time happened. The point man had just passed a row of boulders that were strung across the mountainside when his cover man saw the flash of feathers. The first flash occurred ten yards to the right. Then again, he saw them at about four yards to the right of the point man. The cover man raised his rifle to his shoulder, let out his breath, and the moment the Indian leaped into the path directly behind the man on point, he fired.

The violent encounters occurred across the face of the mountain. Both Indians and troopers were dying. Before the Indians could reach the top edge of the small mountain, the troopers had closed the gap between them to just a couple dozen yards. Unwilling to be captured or surrender, the Indians turned and attacked the troopers, even though they were outnumbered ten to one, at least. Most of the troopers still had loaded rifles, and the twenty or so Indians still alive were within range of not only the troopers on the mountain, but the troopers at the bottom as well.

As the Indians turned and attacked, the major ordered his troopers to fire. There were close to two hundred fifty men repelling the attack. Not all had loaded rifles, but most did. When the Indians turned and charged back down the hill at the troopers, they did so knowing they would die. But their pride and their beliefs would not let them face death by running away from it. They lived by a warrior's code to be brave regardless of how challenging the enemy might be, which meant to take as many enemies as you could into the afterlife with you.

When the troopers fired their volley, a mighty roar echoed up and down the valley. The sound dislodged boulders and sent them tumbling down the mountain into the town and the fort, though they caused little damage. When the smoke cleared, there wasn't one Indian left alive. Tuck eased up to the edge of the mountain top and waved a white cloth over his head. Then he headed down the mountain and around it into the valley to the fort and the town.

CHAPTER FOUR

As Tuck rode through the gate at the fort, Major Jennings blocked his way by standing in the middle of the parade grounds in front of the commander's quarters. Tuck received a long and boisterous ovation from the troopers, who had been waiting for him to ride down off the mountain. Tuck waved before bringing his horse to a stop just short of Major Jennings.

"Hey, Newt, how's it going? Miss me?" Tuck inquired.

"That is Major Jennings, Mr. Tuck," the major replied. "That was you on the mountain back there, wasn't it?"

"It was, Major," Tuck stated.

"Can we talk?" Major Jennings asked.

"Can it wait until morning?" Tuck asked.

"Sure, first thing," the major agreed. "You can use the second-in-command officer's quarters, and get some chow in the same mess as the other day, all right?" Major Jennings offered.

"That'll be fine, Major. Far better than I deserve," Tuck replied.

The following morning, after Tuck had managed to get a few hours of sleep and a hot meal, he met with Major Jennings in his office.

"Morning, Tuck," Major Jennings stated as Tuck stepped into his office. The major was at the map table, studying the map.

"Are you looking for something in particular?" Tuck asked as he crossed the room to the map table. "You can't depend on the maps of the territory for anything other than a basic idea of what you might encounter. These maps were drawn by mountain men with little education, based on memories of travels taken as much as ten years in the past, and by someone other than the individual relaying the information to the mapmaker," Tuck explained.

"That's what I wanted to talk with you about. I'd like to hire you to lead a team of surveyors to create new maps of the territory. You'd be in charge. You'd carry the full weight, power, and privilege due the rank of major."

"You do realize just how big this territory is, right?" Tuck asked.

"Are you saying the job is too big for you?" Major Jennings asked curtly.

"That is a good place to start, Newt," Tuck replied.

"I am Major Jennings, Tuck, not Newt," the major snapped.

"I work better knowing who I'm working with," Tuck replied.

"Calling me by a nickname when I am your commanding officer is disrespectful and invites insubordination. I have earned the right to be addressed as Major or Major Jennings. So I expect to be addressed that way," Major Jennings demanded.

"You are not my commanding officer, Major," Tuck said. Then he turned around and walked out of the office.

"Where are you going? We aren't done here," Major Jennings called after him.

Tuck closed the door behind him, then he marched off the porch. He was halfway to his horse when a guard at the front gate began to bellow. "There's a rider coming. It looks to be a trooper."

Troopers from all over the fort came running to see who the trooper was and hear what he had to say. Everyone gathered around the gate, except the major, who was standing in the doorway to his office. When the trooper rode on through the fort's gate there was a loud collective gasp. The man had been shot with arrows a half-dozen times, and if he hadn't been roped in the saddle, he surely would have fallen off. How the horse managed to find its way back to the fort was totally unclear.

"Get that man off the horse!" the major shouted. Quickly, the trooper was freed and laid on the ground. The post's doctor hurried up to the body to check if the man was still alive. It didn't take long—the doctor only needed a moment to listen for the man's heartbeat and check to see if he was breathing. While he was holding a small mirror under the man's nose, the doc saw a rolled-up rag tucked inside the man's shirt.

The doc pulled out the rag, unrolled it, and found the note inside. He handed the note to a trooper standing nearby and ordered him to take it to the major. The major opened the note, read it, and then read it again.

"Sergeant!" Major Jennings bellowed before reading the note yet again. The sergeant finally broke through the crowd, stepped up, saluted the major, and awaited orders. "Sergeant, find Mr. Tuck and bring him here to my office. If he refuses, shoot him in a non-lethal place. Now, go find him and be quick about it."

Tuck was waiting out by his horse for what he assumed would be a desperate plea for help from Major Jennings and the army. When he saw the sergeant trotting around with a look of panic on his face, Tuck knew he was looking for him. In his frantic search, twice the sergeant glanced past him without seeing him. Tuck found it comical.

After watching the sergeant flounder about for a while, Tuck decided to go to the major on his own. Based on the condition of the courier, he could tell it was critical.

With the sergeant headed for the stables, Tuck headed for the commander's office. He knocked on the door and immediately someone shouted, "Enter!"

Tuck opened the door and the major greeted him with, "I assume you saw the trooper?"

"Kind of hard not to," Tuck replied.

"He had a detailed note rolled up inside his shirt." The major held out the note for Tuck to read.

It was addressed to the major or the officer in charge of the fort. It went on to explain the trek up until two days ago, when the column led by Captain Daniels entered a small valley with steep walls, lots of boulders on the walls, and no vegetation or water. The note said they had scouted the valley before entering and had seen no sign of Indians. So, they moved ahead. The valley, according to the scouts, was just over two miles long. The column was about a quarter mile long and consisted of a hundred twenty-four men and a hundred forty-four animals laden with heavy loads.

Captain Daniels explained briefly how the Indians drove the column farther into the small narrow valley by attacking the rear of the column. As the Indians became more brazen in their attacks, the tighter the column bunched up. Then Indians began to appear at the front of the column. It was during this confusion that Captain Daniels realized they were trapped.

Daniels was unable to determine with any accuracy the number of Indians they were facing. All he could observe was that the mountainside appeared to be covered with Indians.

Daniels then explained the current situation. Twenty-seven troopers dead, fifteen wounded, and they were running out of medical supplies. They were unable to cook and running out of dry food and water, were pinned down among the dead mules and horses, using the supply crates as cover. Dozens of crates were set on fire, Indians attacking randomly throughout the day—five or six times, and at least twice every night. Most men were sleep deprived. *Send help immediately,* the note said. *Don't know if we can hold off for the week it will take for you to arrive, will do best.* It was signed, *Captain Colton Daniels, U.S. Army*

Tuck returned the note to the major and looked at the map. He didn't say anything as he traced his finger over the trail line until he reached a spot where the symbol for mountain was on either side of the trail line.

"Is that where they are?" the major asked.

"I think so, but the only way to know for sure is to go there and see. Unfortunately, Major, they are more than likely already dead," Tuck said without a hint of hope in his voice.

"What? Captain Daniels will never surrender or give up," the major said defensively.

Tuck put his hand up in a faux surrender, and the major stopped talking. Tuck then said, "This pass where they are pinned down is three days away. Even at an around-the-clock forced march, you are two days away. The courier was sent back for help at best three days ago. So, you are looking at a five-day period of constant attacks and dwindling supplies. Even if you were to assemble the troops and supplies to mount a rescue, you won't leave here until late afternoon at the earliest. So, it is now six days before you'll be able to reach them, provided their attackers don't turn and attack you, delaying you even more," Tuck explained.

"I have to send relief. It is my duty to go to their aid," the major stated under his breath as he stared at the map.

"I would think your duty would be to not waste any more men, animals, and equipment," Tuck stated in reply. "Normally, the Indians are not going to let a courier get through unless they have managed to fight their way through. The way the courier was roped to the horse tells me the Indians wanted you to get that note. They want you to lead another column of troopers away from the fort and the town. That way, after you have been gone a day, they can attack the fort and village with overwhelming numbers."

"What am I supposed to do?" the major said in frustration.

"Do your best to determine if they are still alive while risking the fewest number of men," Tuck stated.

"You're one cold bastard," the major growled. "You act as though having sent a hundred men to their death is no big deal."

"It is a big deal, but sending another hundred men to die following the first hundred is a huge deal. I told you not go that way, yet you refused my advice, and that is why those hundred men are dead. It's not my fault, it's yours. Now, do you want to know what I'd do next and why? Or do you want to make yet a bigger mistake and get a lot more people killed?" Tuck barked back at the major.

CHAPTER FIVE

An uneasy silence overtook the pair as each stood staring at the map, not really seeing it. Finally, the major stomped over to his desk, grabbed a cigar and lit it, then walked back over to the table.

"You're right. I should have taken your advice. I need to know what I should do next," Jennings said as he puffed on his cigar.

"Okay, let's give this some thought," Tuck said. Then he ran his finger over the map following several lines in the general direction of the trapped troopers. "The fact that the note states they have been under attack for several days before the courier left to get help tells me something other than an attack on the column is taking place. The Indians are up to something, and I think know what it is."

"And what makes you the expert on the damn savages?" the major snarled.

"Thomas Jefferson, my father, friend, and mentor, was by far the expert on the Indians in the territory. He'd done battle with every tribe, more than once, to survive out here in the wilderness. He spent his entire adult life out here, and I was lucky enough to be taken in by him when my birth parents were killed by Indians. He taught me everything he knew and how to think beyond the moment to what the Indians are planning in the long run. They think beyond the moment to what happens next and then after that. Until you start thinking and planning like the Indians, you are living on borrowed time. You may beat them back in the initial attack, but they will be back to attack again." Tuck spoke with such emotion that it sounded like preaching.

"That's all fine and good, but what are we going to do to rescue the column?" the major asked.

"We're going to play war just like the Indians do. We're going to use deception to give them a false sense of control, and then we'll trap them between the fort and a second column," Tuck said.

"How does trapping them just outside the fort rescue the troopers in the valley?" the major asked.

"All right, Major, here are the details." Tuck grabbed a pencil and started drawing lines on the map. "Captain Daniels took this route," Tuck said, drawing a line roughly following the trail they had talked about five days ago. "These are the trails I believe the Indians took." Tuck drew two lines that went into the mountains that ran along either side of the trail the troopers took.

"Wait, you said there were no trails through the mountains," the major interjected.

"There are no trails!" Tuck snapped. "The only things there are wild game trails—goat and sheep trails."

"Goat trails and sheep trails?" the major asked in disbelief.

"Mountain goat and bighorn sheep trails. Barely big enough for a man to walk single file," Tuck replied.

"You're saying the Indians walk single file for miles in order to navigate through the mountains?" the major asked.

"Now you're just being nasty. How did you ever get to be a major?" Tuck asked sarcastically.

"Don't think being a civilian means I won't have your ass thrown in my jail; I'm perfectly willing and able to do so!" the major threatened.

"If you're gonna do it, have at it. Otherwise, shut up and stop asking stupid questions," Tuck barked. He stood there, staring at Jennings.

Finally, the major said, "Go on."

"These are typically game trails, much too small for our horses to travel easily. The Indian ponies are trained to handle walking these trails. The young braves are taught how to keep their weight at the center point of the animal. This is a great help in following these trails. We don't have the time today to learn how to ride like an Indian. So, the troopers who are part of the rescue will need to walk the trail," Tuck explained.

"So, that's your plan—sneak up on the Indians who took the wild game trails to set up an ambush, and do the same to them?" The major clearly didn't understand where Tuck was taking him.

"No, we will start getting a relief column ready to head out to try and relieve the troopers who are trapped by the Indians. We will ride out from the fort for one day. Then we will split the second column—"

The major once more interrupted him. "We're not going to split our forces. That would be suicide!"

Tuck had enough of the major's negative attitude. "Well, all right then. Good luck. You're going to need it. I'll get with Bonnie and take her as far away as I can before you leave with the second column," Tuck stated and walked toward the door.

"Where the hell are you going?" Jennings asked.

"I've been trying to tell you what I think you need to do, but you just keep doing all you can to belittle me and discount my advice. You've already lost over a hundred men, and if you don't prepare for their next move, you'll lose another hundred-plus men.

Then you'll lose the fort and the town. That's several hundred more men, women, and children who will die unless you can accept that I know what is going on in this territory," Tuck stated in a firm voice.

"Okay, okay. I just have a hard time accepting that someone as young as you knows all this. Before they sent me out here, they sent me to school to learn everything the army knew about the territory and the Indians. It turns out the army doesn't know a damn thing of value in the field. If France decides to invade us, I'm ready and able to defend against them, but now I need you to teach me how to defeat these savages. I'm ready."

"Jefferson didn't teach me to be polite or to worry about how I presented my ideas to others—no sugar with the medicine. He taught me to be honest and direct, so I am. I know it can rub some people the wrong way, but I don't know any other way. We are wasting time, so go call whoever you need to call and have them get the troopers rounded up and ready for bear. Make sure the troopers have at least two hundred shot and enough powder," Tuck instructed. "While you're getting that going, I'll draw out better detail on the map."

Ten minutes later, the major had issued his orders, and Tuck had drawn a dozen new lines on the map.

"It's important that the Indian scouts who are watching us right now buy into the fort sending a second large column out to rescue the first column, leaving a small contingent of troopers to guard the fort and town. The second column is to travel just far enough to lose sight of the fort, but no farther. This is when I believe the Indians will call upon all of their braves to ride with their chief and attack the fort and town," Tuck said.

"But how are we going to help the trapped column farther up the trail?" the major asked.

"The second column will split into two unequal parts. The larger part should consist of approximately three quarters of the troopers, and the second, smaller part will consist of a quarter. The larger portion of the column will stop and send back scouts to see if the Indians took the bait. The larger group will continue moving back toward the fort in order to provide a faster response when the Indians attack the fort."

"Now, I am guessing that the trapped troopers are being controlled by a slight of hand," Tuck stated.

"How's that?" the major asked.

"The Indians have Captain Daniels and his troops pinned down using only maybe two dozen braves. They started out with more, but with each new attack, their numbers get smaller. The Indians are only attacking enough to keep the troopers from getting much rest, forcing them to always be on guard for the next attack," Tuck said.

"You really think there are only a couple dozen braves harassing Daniels and the troop?"

"Yes. I'll take two dozen troopers with me. We'll follow the game trails and come up from behind the Indians. The rest of the second column will be yours to command, and you'll be the hammer that smashes the Indians up against the fort. All that remains is dividing the troops. There needs to be a solid contingent at the fort to defend it. I'll need two dozen barroom brawlers because I expect there will likely be a lot of hand-to-hand combat during the extraction," Tuck said.

"I'll have the sergeant pick the men for you. They might be a little reluctant to volunteer," the major noted.

"They can bitch and whine all they want, as long as they'll fight to the bitter end for their lives. They all need to have a backbone," Tuck said. "Now, while you're getting the parade lined up, I'm going to see Bonnie and make sure she understands what's happening." Tuck walked out to go find Bonnie.

CHAPTER SIX

Tuck went to Bonnie's tent, only to find she wasn't there. He then checked with the general store, the public bath, and the civilian doctor's office. She wasn't at any of them. Tuck was about to give up when he heard a baby crying, and something told him to go to the baby. Sure enough, he rode toward the sound and found Bonnie holding a newborn baby outside the back door of the hotel and poker saloon.

Tuck dismounted and loudly said, "Hey, Bonnie." The sound of Tuck's voice reverberated off the valley walls. Bonnie smiled at Tuck, and Tuck practically swooned.

Bonnie quickly handed the baby to another woman who had attended the child's birth and then ran to Tuck and leaped into his arms.

"I am so glad to see you. I have missed you so much," Bonnie told him as she squeezed his neck so hard that he started to have trouble breathing. Finally she let go of Tuck's neck, put her hands on his face, and kissed him hard on the lips.

"I have missed you, too," Tuck said as he held her close and returned her kiss.

"I didn't know if I should expect you back. You were here the other night but didn't come 'round to see me. What's up with that?" Bonnie inquired.

"I should have, but I got bogged down with the major. The army has a big problem. They sent a column of over one hundred men out to Grand Junction, only they didn't get there. A courier arrived at the fort this morning, dead. He had been tied in his saddle and was carrying a note for the major. The note detailed their situation and asked for reinforcements as soon as possible," Tuck shared.

"So, is the major going to send more troops?" Bonnie asked.

"Yes, but it's tricky. The fastest anyone can reach the trapped column is three days from when they leave the fort. The second column is going to be harassed all the way to the trapped column, which may be a pointless endeavor, as the Indians are attacking the troopers constantly, causing injuries and casualties. The column's supplies are quickly dwindling, and it is just a matter of time until they run out, including ammunition, and the Indians overrun the column," Tuck said.

"Those poor men. Are you leading the relief column?" Bonnie asked.

"This is where it gets complicated," Tuck stated without making eye contact with Bonnie.

"Oh, how so?" Bonnie asked.

"The trapped column is being used as bait," Tuck shared.

"Bait? What do you mean?" Bonnie asked.

"It took the courier at least three days to make it back to the fort. From the description in the note of the Indians' behavior, of how often they were attacking and how many braves were being used in each attack, it's clear they are purposely killing them slowly in an effort to give the soldiers at the fort false hope of saving at least some of them," Tuck explained.

"They are hoping to draw another big column of at least a hundred men from the fort. Once the relief column is far enough away—a full day's march—I firmly believe the Indians will attack the fort and the town in large numbers."

The look on Bonnie's face was one of horror. "What are we supposed to do?" she asked.

"The major is leaving behind a contingent of about sixty men. Plus, he's going to ask every able-bodied man and woman in town to bring their rifles with them and help support the remaining troopers in the fort," Tuck said.

"That'll only provide about another seventy shooters. The Indians are likely to come at us from the mountainside, the forest, the far end of the valley where the mine is scheduled to be dug, and from the front of the fort. How are we supposed to defend all that with maybe a hundred and thirty people?" Bonnie's usual calm was giving way to near panic.

"You have to stay calm, Bonnie. People around here look to you to show them the way. You're their friend and doctor; you're their rock that helps anchor them in the worst storms of their lives. So, you have to take charge and get everyone inside the fort. The column will be turning around at nightfall of the first day out. They will come back and wait just out of sight of the fort for the Indians to make their move. When they do, the major will have to wait until the Indians are fully committed to the attack before he and the second column come racing back and trap the Indians between the fort and column. We're hoping that will be enough to swing the battle over to us," Tuck explained.

"Where are you during all of this?" Bonnie asked.

"I will be with two dozen troopers sneaking up on the Indians that have Captain Daniels and the first column pinned down. We're going in over the mountain on the wild game trails," Tuck said.

"Oh, my God, are you crazy? The Indians are taught from childhood how to walk those trails. Even their horses are taught how to walk those trails. It is only going to take one misstep for men to fall to their deaths. Why are you leading this suicide mission? Why?" Bonnie whined.

Tuck reached out, wrapped his arms around her, and pulled her close.

"I'm leading the counterattack because I'm the only one who can walk those trails. I'm the only one who might be able to find his way forward over those trails because I've lived here for the last ten years, and I am the only one Jefferson taught how to do it. If I don't go, it will mean that many more men will die," Tuck said, holding Bonnie tight.

"Here you go again. You are too damn brave for your own good," Bonnie snapped. "Go on, go save those fools. But don't you get yourself killed, Tuck Tucker. If you do, I will not attend your funeral. I love you. Come back to me, you damn fool." Bonnie walked off, yelling instructions to the townsfolk to hurry up and get up to the fort.

Tuck rode back to the fort and met up with the major. The supply wagons were in place, loaded and ready to go. The double-thick wooden sides of one of the wagons provided some cover for the eight men inside the cargo bed, each armed with three rifles and six loaders.

"We should have everything ready to leave in about fifteen minutes, sir," Sergeant Shaw reported to the major.

"Very good, Sergeant. Before we leave, I want you to post lookouts halfway up the mountainside," the major ordered. "Place them at fifty yards apart, and inform them to keep a sharp eye out for movement up and down the valley and on the mountainsides. Then post two sharpshooters down here at the bottom, the same distance apart. Their job is to watch the backs of the men on the mountainside. Be sure to bring them down before dusk and that you have two men watch the mountainside all night every night. Be sure to string wooden stakes just beyond the trip ropes at dusk tonight, and not before, because we don't want the Indian scouts seeing those lines going out. Be sure to use two-man details to place the trip ropes and leave gaps that our men can pass through safely. Mr. Tuck strongly suggests we set a series of three rope trip lines about four inches off the ground, about eight inches apart." The major instructed the sergeant to do exactly what Tuck said would work well against the sneaky Indians.

Tuck rode up as the sergeant trotted off to get things organized for later. He was pleased to see how the troopers were setting up booby traps for any Indians who might try to sneak into the fort. He had the troopers casually whittle big wooden splinters at the top of the log stockade wall. The troopers cut and partly buried clumps of a dozen wooden spikes in six foot by six foot squares at points that were likely to be seen as good access points for climbing over the wall. The troopers also created rope neck lines, made from strong hemp, with small wooden spikes tied into the line every four inches. Those were set at about five feet eight inches high in low-light areas between the buildings inside the fort. At Tuck's suggestion, they even rubbed saddle soap across the roofs to make them slippery.

"Well, Major Tuck," Major Jennings stated as he walked over to where Tuck sat waiting on his horse, "I have ordered the men to set up booby traps as you suggested and posted the lookouts with sharpshooters in position to watch their backs."

"Nothing is perfect, but all those traps should help slow down the attack and hopefully take some fight out of them," Tuck replied. "I also talked with Bonnie, and she's bringing the townsfolk into the fort shortly."

Robert Hanlon

CHAPTER SEVEN

The townsfolk arrived a few minutes before the major was ready to go. The locals cheered as he took his place at the head of the column, raised his right hand over his head, and bellowed, "Hoooeee!"

Tuck had ridden out a few minutes ahead of the column to scout the trail before the others started down it. As he rode, Tuck didn't make it obvious he was scanning the mountainsides for Indian scouts. He managed to spot just two of them, and they cleared off before Tuck got close enough to engage them. Over the first ten miles, Tuck played hide and seek with the Indian scouts, and the column continued to move forward at a steady pace.

The quarter-mile-long column was scheduled to keep moving, even after dark. In fact, it was essential that they keep moving in order to confuse the Indian scouts. It was a big ruse that would show the troopers making big campfires, setting up tents and cooking racks, only to slip away in the dark. They would meet back down the trail toward the fort and then hurry through the night to be in position at dawn to surprise the attacking Indians.

Tuck and his detail had a slightly more dangerous job the first night out. Their job was to find and kill the two Indian scouts they saw and any others they encountered on the mountainside. They waited for it to be full dark before they, dressed in dark clothes with charcoal on their faces to cut down on reflection, moved up the mountainside on foot.

Tuck led eleven men, and Lieutenant Doleman led the other twelve men. Each detail slowly climbed up the mountainside. They were fanned out twenty paces apart and observing silence to try and keep their climbing a surprise. Below them, the troops made their way to the rendezvous point and quietly walked their horses away from the fake campsite. Tuck crested the mountain first, and he slipped over the edge without making a sound. He moved a few yards from the edge and waited. One of his men reached the top a moment later. He was breathing heavily, and he groaned loudly as he dragged himself over the edge onto the flat mountain top. There were several large boulders on the top, and at first, the man just lay there, trying to catch his breath.

From his spot on the ground a couple of yards away, Tuck saw a shadow move. He saw the brave in the shadow take a couple of steps without making a sound. Then, Tuck saw the brave raise a large knife up over his head. Tuck acted immediately. He leaped up and lunged at the brave with the knife, slamming into him just as he started to lunge toward the trooper who was still flat on his back, catching his breath. As Tuck slammed into the Indian brave, he plunged his knife deep into his throat. The well-placed knife stopped the brave from calling out and severed the main artery in the brave's neck. They rolled across the ground for several yards, and Tuck pushed the body of the brave away from him and over the edge. The Indian's body slid over the loose rocks and sand halfway down the mountain before snagging on an embedded sharp rock outcropping.

Tuck then helped the rest of his men up onto the flattened top of the mountain and ordered them to spread out and search for more Indians. Lieutenant Doleman and his detail didn't fare as well as Tuck's detail had. Tuck's team found and eliminated eight Indian braves. Doleman's team only found three Indian braves, and in the process they lost one of their own men. Once Tuck was sure their work against the Indian scouts was done, he and his men all made it down the mountain to their horses.

"Major Tuck," Major Jennings began, "I'm grateful and impressed. May you have the same success there as you've

experienced here. And may God hold you in the palm of his hand."
Major Jennings looked Tuck in the eye and issued his only order.
"You stay alive, Tuck. That's an order. Now go rescue my men."

"Yes, sir. I'll do my best. Good luck to you as well." Tuck then
did something that confused Jennings. Tuck saluted him, paying
him the respect he had withheld until that moment. Then, Tuck
and his detail rode off into the night.

With Tuck gone, Major Jennings focused on the task before
him and his men—defending the fort.

"Sergeant, let's get moving double time back to the fort and
hope to God, the savages haven't figured out our plan," Major
Jennings both ordered and prayed.

Tuck had to work hard to find the wild game trail in the dark.
He lost half an hour hunting for the trail and vowed to himself to
push the team extra hard, despite the danger, to make up for the
time they lost.

Major Jennings and his one-hundred-man detail moved
swiftly, backtracking over the trail toward the fort. Just before
dawn, the column reached its rendezvous point. Major Jennings
set lookouts and ordered his men to try to get some sleep. Dawn
came and went with no sign of Indians nearby. At mid-morning,
Major Jennings was silently cursing Tuck for obvious reasons.

By mid-afternoon, the troops were surly and downright
grumpy. Major Jennings decided to walk among his men and offer
encouragement.

"Men, are you ready to pull out? We won't have seconds to
spare when the Indians make their move. If you're feeling tired
and run down, I suggest you do some exercises to wake up. This
is just the calm before the storm. Double check your weapons;

make sure the guns are loaded and the knives and tomahawks are honed to the sharpest edge possible. Be sure to eat something, drink plenty of coffee, and then use the latrine. Can't have the damn savages calling us the piss brigade now, can we?" Just as dusk fell, the lookouts both signaled the Indians had finally arrived.

Major Jennings climbed up the back side of the mountain, peeked over the edge of the mountain's crest, and looked out over the plain below. What he saw was startling. If pressed, Major Jennings would have estimated between seven hundred to a thousand Indians just out of cannon range. They had the soldiers outnumbered three to one.

Tuck and his detail made good time as they rode at a steady trot along the wild game trail. It was just before dark when Tuck ordered his men to water their horses and let them rest a few minutes. Tuck was pressing hard to reach the valley where the first column was trapped by dawn. It was a tall order, since they had no idea just how far they had to go to rescue their fellow troopers.

Everyone was watering their horses and eating some hardtack when the first arrow lofted in out of the gathering darkness and struck one of the troopers in the chest. The telltale sound of the arrow hitting its target, the *zip kerplunk,* was the only thing that caught any of the men's attention.

"Indians!" the trooper closest to the slain man bellowed. Every member of their team turned to look at the man who was just killed, as two more arrows came darting, striking another trooper, this one in the back. The third arrow missed everyone by sheer luck, as the trooper who had been targeted dropped to the ground without hesitation. Tuck shouted orders to the remaining troopers to take their time, aim well, and make every shot count.

Of the twenty-two troopers left, all but four managed to see where the Indians were shooting the arrows from and followed Tuck's orders. The eighteen troopers fired in a very tight cluster, and their shots saturated the two places where the Indians were taking cover, killing all three braves. The roar of eighteen rifles firing at approximately the same time echoed up and down the valley they had left, all the way to the watering hole.

"Hurry up! Reload!" Tuck shouted as he directed the four troopers who had not fired their weapons to pay very close attention for any other braves continuing the attack, covering while the others reloaded.

Tuck picked up the arrow that missed its target and studied it. It was a Comanche arrow, not an Arapaho arrow. Once everyone was reloaded, Tuck had each of them take a good look at the arrow and memorize the feather colors.

"Take a good look, gentlemen. Memorize the feather colors and the order of the color rings on the shaft. That pattern will be the same on every arrow, spear, tomahawk, and knife. These arrows belong to the Comanche. They will change slightly, based on which clan they are in. The Comanches will all use the three color stripes in the order you see them here—that signifies the tribe. Then, the two stripes right before the feathers at the rear of the arrow signify the individual clan. If you can remember this, it'll help you deal with the Indians better. They all act differently, though they have common histories and beliefs. Kind of like Scotsmen and Englishmen. They may not get along, but they are similar in their history and basic beliefs." Tuck stopped talking and looked around slowly.

He heard something he believed was the sound of shale slipping and sliding on the mountainside. He made a hand signal, twirling his hand above his head, for the troopers to mount up quickly and quietly, which everyone did. The two troopers killed were tied over their horses' saddles, and the group quickly walked their horses up the trail, using the scattered large boulders to cover their movements.

A minute or so later, seven Indian braves peered over the top of the hill of shale that was next to the watering hole. They looked around, confused by the lack of an enemy or even other members of their clan. There was nothing here to explain the sound of thunder under a clear sky.

After walking a couple hundred yards, Tuck had his men bury the two dead troopers under rocks and mark the map so the bodies might be retrieved later. Then, they mounted their horses and got moving at a near-galloping pace. It was halfway through the night, and they were not yet halfway to the location where the column was trapped.

Meanwhile, Major Jennings was preparing his troops. "Sergeant, you will take half the detail and charge around behind the enemy and then attack from the rear. Fire at least two volleys from a fixed position, so every shot will count. You need to take down as many as possible with those volleys," Major Jennings directed.

"Once you have fired, the other half of the detail will be with me, and we'll fire two volleys from the side of the enemy's position. Then we'll charge them as well. Oh yes, I almost forgot. Have your men reload right away, before you charge. That way, you and your men can fire a third volley before actually engaging the enemy. Make sure everyone fits bayonets before we split up. Any questions?" Major Jennings asked.

"No, sir, it sounds like a well thought out plan. It should cause the savages to think twice before messing with us again," the sergeant said.

"Then let's get to it," the major said as he made his way back down the mountainside.

Robert Hanlon

CHAPTER EIGHT

Just prior to full dark, the Indians built huge bonfires and began dancing around them. They played the drums, beating out a rhythmic melody while chanting loudly.

The major set out skirmish lines, hoping to keep the savages from slipping large numbers of braves out into the darkness and in close to the walls of the fort. About an hour after sunset, two of the men the major had posted to the skirmish line had found an Indian who was pouring animal fat and grease into animal-skin pouches. He then tied the pouches to spears. It was clear the Indians were planning on setting the fort on fire and using the chaos of fire to attack.

"Corporal Neeley, I need four sharpshooters," the major called out.

"Yes, sir," Neely replied. A minute later, he stepped up to where the major was standing. "Sir, the sharpshooters as requested," Neely stated as he saluted. The major slapped down Neeley's hand and barked in the young man's face. "You don't salute me or any other officer in the field. It's a good way to get us killed."

"Sorry, sir," Neeley replied, standing at attention.

"Sorry don't cut it. Now, get those men along the skirmish line about fifty yards out from the fort. They are to shoot the braves carrying spears with skin bags tied to them. If they can shoot the bags, they are to do that as well. Those bags contain grease meant to set the fort on fire. Be sure the sharpshooters have loaders and protectors. Also, be sure these men have at least three rifles and loaders and do their best reloading, helping to defend the sharpshooters. Do you understand, Corporal?" the major snarled.

"Yes, sir, you can count on me," the corporal replied.

The Indians continued to dance, and the cavalry watched. The major was growing steadily more impatient as he was forced to sit in the shadows, waiting for the Indians to make their move. As he stood there waiting, he couldn't help but wonder if Tuck was having any trouble. He wondered if Tuck was still headed toward the doomed column, or if he himself had been ambushed and was now trapped less than ten miles from the first column.

As he approached the doomed column, Tuck had his men fan out across the mountainside. Tuck himself took three troopers with him as he slunk around the campsite, working his way to the best possible path that would lead him to a dozen braves who were sitting around their campfire, planning their next attack on the beleaguered column.

***

"Sergeant, what do you make of that?" Bonnie asked the man in charge.

"I think that is what the scouts call an Indian war dance. It's those damn drums that are driving me crazy, miss," the sergeant said. "Do you have plenty of powder and shot?"

"We have plenty of both," Bonnie replied without turning away from the bonfires and dancing Indians.

"Do you have plenty of water too?" the sergeant asked.

"Oh, yes. I think I counted eight buckets and two sixty-gallon barrels," Bonnie said.

"Now, you should get inside and be prepared for those savages coming over the wall and trying to break in the buildings or setting them on fire," the sergeant told Bonnie.

"Somehow that is not inspiring confidence, Sergeant," Bonnie replied.

"Just the same, miss, you really need to be inside before things start happening. Be sure the women with you know they have to shoot and keep shooting. Otherwise, those savages will find a way in, and far too often, the white women they meet up with—they rape and murder or take them as slaves."

"How colorful, Sergeant. Just tell me I have nothing to worry about and you'll protect me," Bonnie stated with a quiver in her voice.

"I'll do my best, miss. You really don't have anything to worry about until the drums stop," the sergeant stated, and as if he had given them a signal, the drums stopped.

The sudden silence was deafening. A moment later, the war cry of a thousand braves shattered the silence and struck fear deep in the soul of every person who heard it—those inside the fort, and those prepared to engage the savages just outside.

One of the troopers on the wall raced up next to the sergeant and simply blurted out, "They stopped. The drums stopped."

"Get everyone on the wall!" the sergeant shouted. He turned to Bonnie and barked, "Get to your building. Make every shot count." Then the sergeant ran off along the wall, shouting orders as he went.

***

The major shouted to the man next to him, "Get ready, and make every shot count!" Then that trooper passed the message on until every trooper had gotten the message.

The moment the war cry went up, the major shouted, "This is it, boys! Drop those devils!"

The contingent of men along the side of charging Indians held steady. They were to wait until the enemy presented itself in a clear open field. The first line of braves were those carrying spears with the pouches filled with grease. There had to be a hundred braves charging the fort, spears held high over their heads, screaming out their war cry as they raced toward the fort.

The major stood at the ready, his arm held high in the air, his sword clenched tightly in his hand. Braves were thundering across the small plain, racing for the fort. As the braves crossed the halfway point, Major Jennings dropped the hand with the sword, and the troops fired. Fifty rifles exploded, and the lead shot filled the air right as the braves were riding past.

From the wall of the fort, the charging Indians looked a bit like waves upon the ocean, breaking over themselves again and again. The cavalry fired and the fifty musket balls flew, taking down a row of grease-toting braves and splattering the grease across the battlefield. The second line of shooters, assembled seventy–five yards closer to the fort, all took deep breaths and slowly let out the air as they pulled their triggers. Once more, the cavalry made an impact, and another row of savages collapsed, along with their horses, disrupting the charge and scattering the dead, injured, and pouches full of grease across the battlefield.

At least two hundred Indians were down, but from the walls of the fort it hardly seemed to affect the charge or the attack. The Indians were randomly spaced and spread out compared to the ones carrying the fire spears. The major, knowing there was a lot of grease splattered about the battlefield now, instructed a handful of troopers to set fire to the grease. The troopers made a dozen small torches that could be easily tossed fifty to sixty feet. When they were ready, the chaotic charge to the fort was within shooting range, and both sides began shooting at each other. That was when the second column began its surprise attack on the large war party.

Troopers began charging onto the battlefield, giving chase to the savages. Most of the savages had not realized the blue bellies had outfoxed them and were charging down on them from the side and the rear. In most cases, the braves were riding so hard, most seeking revenge for perceived wrongs by the whites, they didn't notice the cavalry until the braves around them and behind them began falling off their horses.

The first wave of Indian braves slammed into the front wall of the fort. Musket balls, arrows, throwing knives, and spears began flying in all directions. It was total chaos—men and animals running aimlessly, first one direction then another, and moments later, yet another direction.

Despite having cut down more than half of the braves in the first wave of the attack, the Indians managed to set fire to the lodgepole. One brave was able to send flaming arrows with large amounts of bear grease into the battlefield. Just as with the grease the Indians had splashed on the walls of the fort, the grease on the battlefield instantly erupted into a scorching inferno.

The fires on the battlefield provided enough light to expose the troopers attacking at the Indians' rear and the side. The change of battle dynamics altered the Indians' plans. What had originally been an offensive battle plan for the Indians now became a defensive plan. Their main goal shifted from destroying the enemy and the fort they were building to a quick escape with as many men still alive as possible.

The Indians left just a small force outside the fort, creating enough of an attack to restrict the troopers inside the fort from leaving. The braves not only forced the troopers on the wall to keep their heads down, but they kept roving bands of troopers and civilians searching the fort for infiltrators.

Small battles were taking place throughout the fort. It was small battles between a dozen men that the Indians excelled at. The Indians had never fought the huge multi-phased battles Europeans had fought over and over since Roman times. They viewed the wholesale slaughter of each other's best hunters and leaders as a waste of the blessings provided by their ancestors and the Great Spirit.

Several buildings had been torched by the attacking braves, and several dozen defenders in the fort were killed, along with even more of the intruding braves. The building that Bonnie and a handful of other women were defending was a fairly large building made of stone. It was big enough that it caught the attention of every brave who stole into the fort. It drew the braves to it, like moths are drawn to flame.

CHAPTER NINE

"Caroline, take your time and aim at what you want to hit!" Bonnie called out over the din of battle.

"They keep moving. If I could just catch one standing still for a minute, I could hit them," Caroline replied.

Bonnie and five other women were shooting through the front windows. The two side windows had been boarded over, inside and out. There were no rear windows, as the army purposely didn't include them in the building plans since it meant to form a section of the fort's outside wall.

"Beth, keep the reloads coming. It looks like the Indians may have overrun the front gate!" Bonnie called. She wasn't seeing any increase in the number of Indians, but fear was a great motivator, and the women in this building were more into hand-wringing than anything else.

"Shoot that savage over by the brig, hurry!" Bonnie called out, and two of the women swung their rifles to the right and fired. One woman shouted gleefully as the brave was knocked back into the wall of the brig and fell to the ground. They could not be positive, but it appeared as though the brave was dead—shot twice—once in the chest and once in the abdomen.

"Ladies, get back, incoming fire arrows!" Bonnie shouted as four arrows came flying through the front windows. The arrows continued all the way to the back wall of the room they were in, setting the wall on fire. The arrows had little pouches of bear grease tied to them, and when they struck the wall, the pouches either burst open or they caught fire. Either way it meant big trouble for Bonnie and the other women.

"We've got to get out of here!" Caroline shouted and headed for the door. Bonnie raced ahead of her from the opposite side of the room and stopped her from opening the door.

"We can't just open the door. There are a dozen Indians out there waiting for us to do just that!" Bonnie shouted over the roar of the flames. The other fifteen women in the building all began crowding around the door, pushing Bonnie into the door.

"I want out. I don't want to burn alive in here!" Mary, one of the reloaders, cried out. Bonnie knew she had to do something and do it fast.

"Are all the guns reloaded?" Bonnie asked.

"I think so," Mary replied as two arrows came flying in the windows. One arrow struck Betty in the chest, and the other arrow flew harmlessly into the back wall.

"Quick, give me the powder horns!" Bonnie shouted. Within ten seconds, Bonnie had all twelve of the powder horns. "Everybody get down on the floor in the corner." Bonnie directed the women to the far left front corner of the building. "Get down on the floor and cover your faces, hurry!" she shouted.

She tossed four of the powder horns against the far right wall, about halfway back toward the rear of building. Then she dropped to her knees, far into the corner with the other women.

KABOOM! BOOM! The four powder horns exploded, taking most of the wall with them. There had been a large number of Indians hiding against that wall on the outside of the building, and now they were dead Indians. The dozen or so braves out in front of the building couldn't control themselves. They were all worked up, and after the wall was destroyed by a couple of powder horns, they had become reckless.

"Caroline, throw a couple of those powder horns out front," Bonnie directed.

Caroline balked. She froze in place, terrified and disabled by fear. "I'm not getting anywhere near the door. Those savages are coming for us. Where are our men?"

Undaunted, Bonnie was not about to go down without a fight. She grabbed the powder horns from Caroline and flung them out the front door. Then she shouted, "Shooters, point your guns at the door and get ready to fire!"

Suddenly, there were blood-curdling screams outside, and Bonnie fired at the two powder horns she'd just tossed outside. She missed, allowing several braves to charge the building.

"Shoot, ladies, shoot!" Bonnie ordered. The women with guns fired, though not quite in unison. A couple of the braves were hit, but four more continued, unabated, to the door.

Bonnie reached for another rifle, one that had been reloaded, and found Caroline right there handing her the gun. Bonnie swung it around fast, and with little effort to aim, fired. This time she hit one of the powder horns and it exploded, setting off the second powder horn.

Three of the four braves took the impact from the double blast of the exploding powder horns directly and were killed. The fourth one, however, was driven forward through the door and lay sprawled across the floor inside the building. Bonnie had also been struck by the shock wave and knocked backwards into a desk. She was barely conscious. When the brave gathered his wits about him, he looked up and saw Bonnie, with her pretty face and flaming red hair, just a few feet in front of him. He scrambled to his feet, pulled his knife, and started toward Bonnie. He was intent on scalping her, because he'd never seen red hair before, and having a red-haired scalp on his lodgepole would bring him great prestige.

Just as he was about to grab Bonnie, a rifle butt came flying in from the far right, striking the brave upside the head, and dropping him where he stood. When the brave's body struck the floor, his attacker, Caroline, continued to pummel his head until all that remained was a bloody puddle on the floor.

Bonnie was helped up, and all the women hurried out of the burning building. They went across the street to the brig, and the troopers there graciously invited them in. Together they fended off the savage intruders.

Meanwhile, outside the post, Major Jennings was trying hard to deliver a truly fatal blow to the savage attackers. He had his men dismount. Rather than chase the Indians, he ordered his men to form battle lines, three rows of twenty men each, standing one behind the other.

The firing square worked like this: the first row would fire, then reload while the second row fired. Then, the second row reloaded, and the third row fired. Then the rotation repeated. With approximately two hundred men, the major was able to create three firing squares, and their effect was devastating on the Indians. With each line's firing, anywhere from fifteen to twenty braves fell.

At first, the Indians didn't realize they were facing more than the return fire from the fort. When it was realized they were being shot at from four different directions, the word "ambush" began flowing freely across the battlefield, and the Indians began escaping to the north-northwest along the White River.

The major was pleased by his men's response in a crisis. They had really stepped up, following orders and finding new and creative ways to complete their orders. As the Indians escaped, dozens of troopers gave chase, only to have the major counter their enthusiasm by signaling recall. As the major sat there in his saddle, he took stock of the carnage before him.

There were dozens of small fires burning across the battlefield. The bodies of their savage antagonists and the brave defenders of the fort and town were spread over the battlefield and grounds of the fort. There were buildings, along with large sections of the fort's wall, that had been reduced to cinders.

Despite the element of surprise and the overwhelming fire power of the cavalry, the savages were not alone in suffering grave losses. Intermixed with the bodies of the savages lay the bodies of nearly one hundred troopers. Inside the fort were several dozen savages, and just as many or more troopers and civilian defenders who had been killed in the attack.

The wounded numbered around two hundred, and they were laid out across the front of the commander's office, the officers' mess, and the officers' quarters. The army's doctor was overwhelmed, even with the help of four privates. After recall was sounded, Bonnie and the women in the brig ventured out and began assessing the damage and loss of life. As they walked past the officers' mess, now serving as the fort hospital, Bonnie couldn't help but feel she needed to help. She wasn't going to ignore that feeling.

"Ladies, our jobs are not finished yet. I need you to go around to the wounded and tend to their wounds. You need to do your best to stop the bleeding. Be sure to talk sweetly to the wounded; your voice may be the last voice they hear," Bonnie said.

"Now, there are a lot of wounded men here, so don't just help one man. Help as many as you can. Keep moving, but don't let any of them feel like they are alone. If you need me, I'll be in with the doctor." Bonnie handed her gun to Caroline, then she walked briskly into the officers' mess.

Major Jennings, after reviewing the battlefield, knew exactly what was needed. "Corporal Neeley," he bellowed, "form four, four-man squads with shovels. We need to burn all these dead bodies."

"Yes, sir, right away, sir," the corporal replied as he tried to trot off before hearing all he needed to hear in order to carry out his order.

"Stop, Corporal, stop right there. You don't even know what I want you to do," the major barked. "Dig a pit, ten feet round, four feet deep. Fill the pit with bodies and burn them. Use kerosene to get the fire burning. Make up four pits, so you won't have to drag the bodies very far. When you've finished burning the bodies, fill in the pits, and make them as level as possible. In other words, spread out the dirt so the pit isn't so noticeable. You understand my instructions, Corporal?"

"Yes, sir. Dig pits, burn the bodies, and cover the pits with the dirt we dug out, spreading the dirt, so exactly where we burned and buried them is unclear," Corporal Neeley confirmed.

CHAPTER TEN

Tuck directed his men with hand signals until all twelve in his detail were lined up behind boulders in the dark. Several dozen yards away, Lieutenant Doleman and his group were spread out across the mountainside about a third of the way up. They were there to protect the backs of Tuck's men and to act as reinforcements, if needed.

The Indians appeared to be overconfident. They had trapped over a hundred men to start this fracas, and now, after a week when they had been able to attack and kill as many as they wanted when they wanted, it no longer seemed possible to them that the captives could or would do more than put up a minimum defense. They were directed by their chief to end this waste of time and resources the next day. Then they were to prepare to spearhead the attack on the second column of blue bellies. They expected little or no resistance. These blue bellies didn't seem to know how to fight or to defend their position. The number of blue bellies they had trapped below had slowly been whittled down with each attack, until now there were fewer than a dozen who were uninjured, and they were in need of food and water.

Tuck and his men had seen the smoke from the Indians' fire and smelled the roasted lamb they had killed and cooked for their evening meal. From where Tuck was watching, he could see they weren't unlike white men. They laughed and joked, argued, danced, challenged each other, and even cared for each other, as witnessed by the effort given to one of their group who was injured. Tuck hadn't been taught by Jefferson that Indians were just like him. Jefferson had said they were dangerous, small-thinking creatures, only slightly smarter than a bear or a horse. What Tuck saw around this campfire told a different story. All the same, they had to die; they had kidnapped and been slowly killing troopers for fun.

Tuck's men were spread out in a half circle, and each one had a clear shot at one of the ten braves sitting around the fire waiting for the meat to finish cooking. Tuck was about to give the signal to fire when four more braves suddenly emerged from the darkness. Just like when a white man met up with his friends at the saloon, the Indians greeted each other. Then, one of the newcomers pulled out his knife, and despite the heat, carved off a big chunk of lamb.

That move was met with anger and indignation as the others complained about the brave's manners. Tuck quickly raised his hand, gave his team a moment to get prepared again, and then he dropped his hand. Eleven rifles fired at once, and a twelfth rifle fired a split second later. All twelve of the braves around the fire were shot dead.

Two of Tuck's men started to approach the fire, when Tuck called out, "Fall back now. Don't go into the light. Fall back."

The man closest to Tuck followed Tuck's order and quickly retreated farther into the darkness, but the other man continued toward the fire. When he got there, he quickly scoured the bodies, looking for anything of value. He found a small number of coins, several well-made knives, and some beaded pieces of Indian jewelry.

At the bottom of the hill, Tuck confronted the fool. "I gave you an order, soldier," Tuck stated in a harsh whisper.

"You ain't no real soldier. You're just some scout the major hired because some dumbass captain has gotten himself captured by the enemy. I only take orders from real soldiers," the trooper said.

"I see," Tuck replied. "I don't give a donkey's ass what you think is real or fake. You were given an order, and you were to follow that order immediately. Now, empty your pockets and then get to your post," Tuck ordered.

"Go to hell. I don't take orders from civilians," the trooper said as he walked over to his horse and started stuffing things in his saddlebags.

Tuck walked over to the trooper and spun him around. Then, in one smooth move, he delivered a solid punch to the trooper's gut. The blow doubled him over, and Tuck delivered a sweeping right hook, smashing his fist into the trooper's face, knocking him backwards several steps before he landed on his back, out cold. Tuck looked at a nearby trooper and barked, "Tie this fool on his horse where he can't untie himself. Make sure he is tied down securely, and that a trooper is with him at all times."

Tuck then lit a torch and began searching through the rocks and underbrush for survivors from the first column. It was tough going. Most of the men were dead and in various states of decay.

The land consisted of a series of wide natural steps that descended from each side of the valley, forming a big v-shaped valley and a natural funnel. Tuck knew the steps were a sign of regular flash flooding, and they offered little in the way of a natural defensive position. In Tuck's mind, they could not have chosen a worse place to make a stand, and the number of dead men scattered about confirmed it.

Tuck's team climbed all the way down, about twenty feet. At the bottom was a small stream, with a trickle of water carving a channel through the rock a quarter inch at a time. They found a group of troopers huddled together in the darkness, pointing their rifles at them. No one said a word. The troopers simply sat there, their eyes wide with fear, their bodies trembling. Finally, Tuck spoke.

"I'm Major Tucker, Tuck for short, and I'm here to help you. I need you to come with us right now. It isn't safe here," he said calmly. As he reached out his hand, several of the men pulled the triggers of their rifles. There was no explosion signaling the guns having fired, just a loud clicking sound, then silence.

It took a few moments for the terrified troopers to react, and their reaction wasn't what Tuck had expected. They, en masse, broke down and cried. It wasn't a few tears that fell. It was more along the lines of full-out blubbering. As Tuck's men helped the others out of their cubbyhole in the side of the riverbank, they too became overwhelmed with emotion. Between the amount of emotion being exhibited and the frail condition of the troopers after their ordeal, extracting them was anything but quick. The slow-motion rescue was about to become a second siege.

Dawn broke, and the last few stragglers were just then starting to mount their horses. That was when Tuck saw Captain Daniels. His left arm was in a makeshift sling, and he had a bandage wrapped around his head. It was clear from the look on the man's face he was in very rough shape. At first, Tuck wanted to say he deserved what he got, "Pride goeth before the Fall," and all that, but the longer he looked at him, the more he could see that Daniels was a broken man. The price for this mistake was too high for him to bear. Slowly, Tuck's disdain for the man faded to pity. His wounds may heal, but the mental scars probably never would. Plus, what had been a promising career was now, in all likelihood, over.

"Let's go, people, we're wasting daylight," Tuck called out as the last of the defeated troopers mounted up. He put Daniels out of his mind; he still had to get these men home.

The second half of Tuck's rescue detail was slowly moving out of the valley when a handful of arrows came flying in from a tree-filled boulder field to the left of the slow-moving column. There were only five arrows, and only three of the five managed to hit their targets. The trooper who had refused to take orders from a civilian was struck in the back by an arrow and died. The horse he was on was also hit by one of the arrows, causing it to go lame. The third arrow hit its mark when it struck Tuck in his thigh. He was lucky. It hit the outer edge of his thigh, missing all major arteries and veins.

Tuck, along with the rest of troopers, quickly dismounted. A few men returned fire. The arrows kept coming, although much more sporadically.

"Can anybody see them?" Tuck called out as he busted off the arrow in his leg and pulled out the two pieces—one from the front and one from the back.

"No, sir," was the collective reply.

"Keep a sharp eye, gentlemen, it is the only way we can hope to spot them," Tuck directed. "You may shoot at will," he added to be sure no one failed to shoot any Indian they saw. "Corporal Brose, I need you," Tuck called to one of the men. "Get a good-sized bandage with extra padding for both front and back, then come back here and wrap my leg. Now, go get the bandages." Tuck dismissed him and called for Lieutenant Doleman.

"Yes, sir, what can I do for you? How's the leg?" Doleman asked.

"Not too bad. It's a through-and-through. Brose is going to bandage it for me, and then we need to get moving," Tuck said.

"Any suggestion as to how we might be able to do that?" Doleman asked.

"I need you to pick six men to accompany you and the men from the first column on the rest of the trip back to the fort. The rest of us will find the Indian raiders who are dogging us," Tuck said. "Arm everyone who can still handle a weapon," he added.

"Yes, sir, but why would we split our forces?" Doleman asked.

"'Cause if we stay here, they'll gradually pick us off until we're all dead. So, we need to put the pressure on the raiders. By splitting up, they'll have to deal with us chasing them before they can begin chasing you."

"So, you and the majority of the able-bodied men are going to fight a delaying action in an effort to buy us time to escape?" Doleman clarified.

"There you go. You understand. Now, get everyone ready, but wait until I start the men moving uphill. Then you mount up and take off; go as fast as you can," Tuck said.

"Sir?" Doleman asked.

"Yes?" Tuck replied.

"Well, sir, you're injured," Doleman said.

"And you think because I'm slightly injured I should go with the injured and leave the direct fight to you and the other troopers who have yet to be injured?" Tuck was not gracious in accepting his underling's support and concern.

"Well, sir, it's just that the savages are in such good condition, it would be a disadvantage for you to have to fight while injured," the lieutenant stammered.

"Doleman, you're a fine soldier, and you may one day become a fine Indian fighter, but as of right now, I'm your best hope of surviving the next three days—wounded or not. So, lead the wounded down the trail, and I'll stay behind and direct our rear action. You have one job, and that is to keep moving. I want you to push your charges to breaking point and beyond. No sleep, no stopping for more than a quick watering of the men, horses, and the brushes, understand?" Tuck asked.

"Yes, sir, I understand," Doleman answered, as Brose finally returned with bandages.

A few minutes later, a couple of troopers risked their lives to draw the fire from the enemy. They ran between two different sets of boulders at opposite ends of the area where the troops had taken cover. Nothing happened. Tuck signaled a second set of troopers to do the same thing as the first. There were at least twenty rifles pointed up the side of the mountain in the same general direction. This time, four arrows flew.

The four arrows zipped through the air, narrowly missing the troopers, but providing targets for the riflemen to shoot at. The rifles fired in chaotic fashion as the troopers were told to fire at will. The Indian archers were fast and fairly accurate. Somehow, they were able to just pop up and fire their arrows and hit or narrowly miss their intended targets before dropping back down amid the boulders.

Corporal Brose watched the game the Indians were playing and began to wonder aloud. "Mr. Tuck, they are right fast. How are we ever going to shoot them when they keep changing their positions and only stand up long enough to lose an arrow at us?"

"Corporal, they'll get tired or run out of arrows, and that is when they'll make the mistake of trying to raid us for weapons. It means we have to stay awake at all times, but we'll get them sooner or later." Tuck tried to be encouraging, but it wasn't a very good pep talk.

"Tuck," one of the other troopers called out, "we've got at least twenty braves running up the riverbed coming toward us. What should we do?"

Tuck looked upstream, and all he saw were rocks—big rocks and boulders. The mountainside was covered with loose rock, with large stones and boulders mixed in. Tuck called out to the sentry, "How far out are those twenty braves?"

"About a hundred yards," the sentry replied.

"Okay, get down, and get ready to shoot any Indian you see as soon as you see him. Brose, go find me six to ten powder horns and some cloth to wrap them in," Tuck directed.

Brose just stood there, looking at Tuck.

"Go get the items I asked for," Tuck pushed.

"Oh, yeah, right, ten powder horns and cloth to wrap them in?" Brose slowly turned away and Tuck was over it.

"Corporal, move your ass, or I'll save the Indians the trouble and shoot it off myself," Tuck snarled.

"Yes, sir." Brose raced off and Tuck brought eight more troopers over to watch the riverbed.

Just as Brose was returning with the items, the twenty extra braves arrived and sent a volley of twenty arrows into their little camp. Several troopers were hit, a couple of them killed. The returned rifle fire killed some of the new attackers, but it was hard to tell how many.

While the battle raged on, Tuck, Brose, and two other troopers wrapped the powder horns and dribbled kerosene over one end of them. Tuck had Brose and the other two troopers take a couple of the makeshift bombs, then they spread out along their battle line. They were to light the kerosene-soaked cloth and then toss the powder horns as far up the mountainside as they could. Everyone was to provide covering fire as soon as Tuck signaled them to begin tossing the bombs.

"We want to toss these powder horns as far up the mountainside as possible. We want to cause a rock slide. I want you to toss yours up above where the raiders were first seen. I'll be tossing mine above the group on the riverbed. Count to five and let them fly," Tuck told the troopers. Then he dashed toward the group of Indians in the riverbed. Each man already had a small fire in which to dip the bombs, and on the count of five, they started flinging them as far as they could up the mountainside.

Tuck tossed the first one directly at the spot where the braves had taken cover. The second one he threw up the opposite side of the riverbed, and he was pleased to see a brave tossed in the air by the explosion. He then turned and tossed the remaining three bombs up on the mountainside.

The noise of the closely timed explosions sounded a lot like rolling thunder during one of the nasty spring storms that sprang up over the mountains. It took several seconds for most of the combatants to regain their hearing, and the silence was deafening. The troopers were instantly discouraged, but Tuck knew better, because he had mined minerals with Jefferson doing exactly what they had done here. Every time, there would be an explosion, followed by short calm before the rocks began moving. It was no different here.

"Wait for it," Tuck shouted, and he ducked behind a huge boulder, flattening himself against it. The troopers followed his example.

The rock slide started as a low rumble and a few smaller rocks tumbling down a few yards. Then there was a loud crack, and a good-sized boulder, probably weighing a thousand pounds, began sliding. It rolled, picking up speed, and a moment later it crashed into another large boulder. The slide was on.

Tuck yelled, "Take cover!" as the mountainside let loose and hundreds of tons of rocks came racing down. The troopers were all on the lee side of large boulders, while the Indians were on the exposed side of similar boulders much higher up the mountain. The closeness to the start of the slide didn't give them a chance to escape to relative safety as even some of the largest boulders slid as well.

The sound of the slide was much, much louder than anyone expected. The roar lasted much, much longer as well. Instead of tossing a few small stones and dust in the air, the slide sent stones of all sizes and small rocks in every direction. It kicked up enough dust to darken the sky over the valley. There was so much dust in the air it became difficult to breathe. All the troopers were coughing and gagging as they helped each other stagger away from the slide area.

Corporal Brose found Tuck clinking to the backside of a boulder, standing in two feet of loose shale and sand. Around the boulder, the gaps between it and the other boulders were all filled deeper than a man was tall. Tuck was lucky to be alive, and he welcomed Brose's slaps on his back to loosen the dust so he could cough it up and out.

Tuck and Brose were the last two troopers to leave the slide zone. They had lost three more troopers in the slide, bringing their total losses to ten men. The Indians appeared to have lost everyone. There wasn't a single arrow fired to hinder their escape up the trail. Tuck felt good about the situation, having rescued the survivors of the first column, though having lost ten men in doing so. It had been a high cost to pay. Tuck knew the battle wasn't over—they still had to keep moving for thirty-six hours to reach the fort. He doubted the Indians would allow them to return peaceably to the fort; too many braves had been sacrificed.

Tuck pressed the troopers to make up the five hours they had lost fighting the delaying action. They kept a steady pace, pushing the horses to gallop whenever the terrain allowed and maintaining a steady trot the rest of the time. They rode on through the night without stopping for anything more than to water and feed the horses and feed themselves. Each stop took no longer than ten minutes.

Back at the fort, Major Jennings had put half the post to work building a bigger and stronger wall, including two ramparts upon which he posted the cannon and made room for a second one. Cleaning up the battlefield proved to be far tougher and take far longer than he had anticipated. He increased the detail to three times the size he had assigned to it originally. Now, as they entered the third day after the battle, it appeared as though they'd be finished burning bodies by the end of the day.

They had lost three buildings to fire. The major assigned a small detail to start clearing the burned and damaged lumber from the sites and begin rebuilding them. While supervising the rebuild of the wall, Major Jennings climbed up on the wall to get a better view of the progress on the battlefield. He had been alone with his thoughts for several minutes, watching the men work, before Bonnie walked up and stood next to him.

The major seemed to be annoyed by her presence. "Miss Bonnie, is there something I can help you with?"

"Not unless you can tell me Tuck will be riding in here shortly, and that he's in fine shape and uninjured," Bonnie replied. "Oh, I know, if anyone can rescue those troopers, it's Tuck. But it's been a week, and he hasn't come back yet."

"I've sent small patrols to search for any sign of the detail, but they have found nothing so far." Major Jennings tried to console her, but it was hard to compete against a man like Tuck. On one hand, he admired Tuck, and on the other, he hated the guy with a passion.

"I can't help but think how big of a waste of life all this is. The braves are truly brave and fearless. The troopers are terrified but well trained and couldn't run from the fight no matter what the cost might be. Then there is Tuck. He's a combination of both— he's the good and the bad. He's fearless and courageous. He's stubborn as a mule, if it matters, as in life and death. He's generous and will never turn away a stranger in need, and he never shies away from a fight," Bonnie said.

"Whoa, there. Why are you telling me how great you think Tuck is? It sounds as if you're trying to convince yourself," the major replied, not making eye contact.

"Oh, I know how great he is. Believe me, I know," Bonnie said.

"Then what are you going to about it?" the major asked.

"What am I go to do?" Bonnie mumbled. She spun around and trotted down the rampart. "What am I going to do about it?" Bonnie was shouting loudly as she stomped across the compound. "You'll see what I'm going to do. You'll see."

***

Tuck and his detail crested the hill, and before them, no more than a thousand yards, was the other part of their detail. They were walking at a slow but steady pace. To a man they were slumped in their saddles, as if they were positioned that way and tied to their horses.

"I told you we'd catch up about this time—mid-afternoon, the second day," Tuck stated as he beamed with pride having correctly guessed the timing.

"Tuck, we've got company!" Brose bellowed from the far end of the line. "They're coming in from the far left. I count thirty braves."

Sure enough, off to the far left was a band of an Arapaho war party. They were somewhere around two or three hundred yards closer than Tuck's detail was, and they outnumbered Tuck's detail three to one.

"Form a skirmish line and charge!" Tuck bellowed. His detail quickly formed up as they charged across the open ground toward the other part of the detail, hoping to help ward off the Indians charging from a different angle.

Lieutenant Doleman closed ranks the moment he became aware of the Indians. As the Indians closed on the detail, Doleman led the men to the nearest rock outcropping and set up defensive positions. One of the troopers pointed out the small group of troopers charging toward them, but there were only about a dozen troopers coming to their aid.

"Hold your fire until they're close enough for you to see their eyes. Make every shot count," Doleman commanded. Even though he'd been under fire for the past week, Doleman's stomach was doing flip-flops as he watched the savages close in on his position. The troopers in the distance weren't going to reach them in time. The ten men with rifles had to defend against thirty of the enemy.

At a hundred yards out, the braves began whooping and hollering. Doleman and the troopers didn't have to be told the odds; it was clear the price they were about to pay, but not one man broke ranks and ran.

"Steady! Hold your fire. Steady!" Doleman directed his men.

Tuck was still seven hundred yards away when the Indians swept over the detail. Doleman and his troops would be on their own for at least five minutes before he could intervene. Tuck felt hopeless and useless as he continued to ride all out.

The braves let loose a volley of arrows when they closed inside fifty yards.

"Fire!" Doleman bellowed, and the troopers fired as one. The braves were so close, every shot hit a target, and chaos erupted. Ten braves fell in the rifle volley, as did more than a dozen troopers, most of whom were already injured in the siege of the column headed for Grand Junction.

The braves were on top of the detail in a flash. There hadn't been time to reload, so the fighting devolved into hand-to-hand combat. Tomahawks, knives, rifle butts, spears, and swords slashed and hurled through the air. Blood and guts flowed across the dry sandy soil, turning the white sand pink.

Tuck and his men arrived at a full gallop. They each fired their rifles with deadly accuracy. Then, they too joined in the up close and personal, life and death struggle. When the dust cleared and the cost was tallied, only the devil had won that day. Twenty-eight savages were killed with two wounded braves escaping in the chaos. Twenty-one more troopers were killed. All but five were members of the ill-fated first column detail. Braves had run through the injured, stabbing and slicing as they went. Lieutenant Doleman had been killed by an arrow to his chest. Corporal Brose had died from a blow by a tomahawk to both his back and his gut. Captain Daniels had fought off four Indian braves before a fifth killed him with a spear in his back.

Tuck had ripped open his wounded thigh, but he had brought down three braves just the same. It took the survivors two hours to collect the dead and tie their bodies on their horses. The detail then continued on to the fort, arriving mid-morning the next day.

Robert Hanlon

CHAPTER ELEVEN

Tuck led the detail into the fort with the entire company turned out to witness the bittersweet homecoming. Although they would call it a successful mission, they still lost nearly three quarters of both details. Of the one hundred forty-eight troopers between the column one detail and the rescue detail, one hundred eight troopers had been killed.

Tuck rode up to the commander's office and was met by Major Jennings, the fort's doctor, and Bonnie, who was running up the trail to the fort from town.

"Welcome back, Tuck," the major stated as he stuck out his hand to shake.

The doctor mumbled as he stepped up and immediately began checking over Tuck's numerous small cuts and puncture wounds. When he reached Tuck's thigh wound, he became extremely concerned.

"Major, I need to get Mr. Tuck on my surgery table as soon as possible. He has a badly infected wound on his thigh, and growing infections on his left shoulder and right center of his gut."

"Hold on there, Doc. I've had worse injuries, and besides, I was in the middle of giving the major my report. So, go get things ready for me, and I'll be in when I've finished my report," Tuck snapped.

"Your wound is bleeding; that is not a good sign. I need to get to work on you right away. I don't know how you're standing on it," the doc asserted.

"Doc, it hardly hurts at all," Tuck said.

"What's not a good sign?" Bonnie asked as she appeared next to Major Jennings.

"Bonnie!" Tuck exclaimed and tried to step over to her, but he stopped when the pain flared in his thigh, registering as a large grimace on his face.

Bonnie stepped up to Tuck and kissed him. "You better not be dying, Tuck Tucker. If you go and die on me, I will dig you up and shoot you myself," she snarled, grabbing his hand. "Major, if you want to talk with him, you'll need to come along and do it while I work." Bonnie commandeered the medical quarters.

Tuck was just as surprised as the others. Everything happened so quickly, all he could do, aside from lash out physically, was to give the major a pleading look as she dragged him away.

"Major, she can't do that. The fort's medical quarters are off limits to everyone who is not army medical personnel!" the doc objected loudly.

The major's response was simple and straightforward.

"She just did."

The End

Printed in Great Britain
by Amazon

75713664R00047